Tea FOR Ruby

by

SARAH FERGUSON
THE DUCHESS OF YORK

illustrated by

ROBIN PREISS GLASSER

A Paula Wiseman Book
Simon & Schuster Books for Young Readers
New York   London   Toronto   Sydney

To Beatrice and Eugenie—
you make my world complete
—S. F.

For Jacqueline Preiss Weitzman—
my sister, my partner, my friend
—R. P. G.

SIMON & SCHUSTER BOOKS FOR YOUNG READERS • An imprint of Simon & Schuster Children's Publishing Division • 1230 Avenue of the Americas, New York, New York 10020 • Text copyright © 2008 by Sarah Ferguson, The Duchess of York • Illustrations copyright © 2008 by Robin Preiss Glasser • All rights reserved, including the right of reproduction in whole or in part in any form. • SIMON & SCHUSTER BOOKS FOR YOUNG READERS is a trademark of Simon & Schuster, Inc. • Book design by Dan Potash • The text for this book is set in Fiddlestix. • The illustrations for this book are rendered in ink, watercolor, and colored pencil. • Manufactured in the United States of America • 10 9 8 7 6 5 4 3 2 1
Library of Congress Cataloging-in-Publication Data • York, Sarah Mountbatten-Windsor, Duchess of, 1959– • Tea for Ruby / Sarah Ferguson, The Duchess of York ; illustrated by Robin Preiss Glasser. — 1st ed. • p. cm. • "A Paula Wiseman book." • Summary: As Ruby tells everyone about her invitation for tea with the Queen, family and friends remind her about how she should conduct herself. • ISBN-13: 978-1-4169-5419-4 (hardcover : alk. paper) ISBN-10: 1-4169-5419-8 (hardcover : alk. paper) • [1. Etiquette–Fiction. 2. Kings, queens, rulers, etc.–Fiction. 3. Afternoon teas–Fiction.] I. Preiss-Glasser, Robin, ill. II. Title. • PZ7.Y823Te 2008 • [E]–dc22 • 2007045350

You are invited
to have tea with
The Queen
on Sunday.

Please bring your very best manners.

"the Queen."

"I've been invited to have tea with the Queen!"

"Ruby, I hope you won't interrupt when you have tea with . . .

"The Queen."

The Queën."

"I've been invited to have tea with the Queen!"

"Ruby, I hope you will dress appropriately when you have tea with . . .

The Queen."

"The Queen"

Oops

"Ruby, I hope you won't talk when you shouldn't when you have tea with . . .

"The Queen."

"The Queen."

"Ruby, I hope you won't talk with your mouth full and won't tip your chair back and will use your fork and napkin when you have tea with . . .

"Tomorrow I'm having
tea with the Queen!"

"Ruby, I hope you'll remember to sit up
straight when you have tea with the Queen."

Today's the day!

"Let's hurry so we won't be late!"

Remember to chew with my mouth closed.

Remember not to speak with my mouth full.

Remember to say "please" and "thank you."

Remember to welcome people.

Remember to use my fork and napkin.

Remember not to interrupt.

Remember not to shout.

Remember to wait my turn.

Remember to sit up straight.

Remember not to talk when I shouldn't.

"GRANDMA?"

"May I offer you more tea, Princess Ruby?"

"Oh, yes, please, Grandma. Thank you."

Dear Grandma,
Thank you so much
for inviting me to
use
ted. I tried to have
my very best manners.
The tarts were delicious
but my favorite thing
was just being with
you! I Love you,
Ruby